Tilly

takes a

Curtain...

Caroline Plaisted

Illustrated by Hollie Jacobs

Catnip

CATNIP BOOKS
Published by Catnip Publishing Ltd
14 Greville Street
London EC1N 8SB

This edition first published 2012
1 3 5 7 9 10 8 6 4 2

Text © 2012 Caroline Plaisted
Illustrations © 2012 Hollie Jacobs
The moral rights of the author and illustrator have been asserted.

A CIP catalogue record for this book is available from the British Library.

ISBN 978-1-84647-143-8

Printed in India by Replika Press

www.catnippublishing.co.uk

Remembering Nancy Robinson

Chapter One

Something exciting was happening at the Grand Theatre, I could tell. Like every Saturday morning, I was there for Extras. Extras is a special ballet class I go to with my best friend Rose. It's held in the dance studios of the Grand Theatre, with a teacher of the Grand Ballet!

This Saturday, my mum and dad dropped me at the Stage Door. They're both dancers with the Grand Ballet. As I walked to the changing room, I could see groups of dancers huddled together, talking and grinning.

What was going on? I wondered. Mum and Dad hadn't said anything to me. And when I entered the studio for the start of class, Miss Marion, our teacher, was just the same as she always is. She was standing at the front looking super smart, her feet turned out in a perfect first position.

Miss Marion used to be a dancer and she's quite strict. She's not unkind, but she expects us to concentrate and work hard.

'Ready, boys and girls?' she smiled. 'Then let's start.'

I'm never sure which bit of class I like best. At the beginning, when you're at the *barre*, you know you're preparing your body so it will be strong enough to do the centre work. But when you get to the centre and have the chance to face the mirror at the front of the studio, you're practising what it will be like to be on stage. So it's hard to decide – I love every bit of my class!

This Saturday, we did lots of centre work. We danced to tunes from *The Nutcracker, Sleeping Beauty, Cinderella* and even *Swan Lake*. Miss Marion made us laugh when we did a jumping routine. She said we sounded like a herd of elephants rather than elegant swans gliding across a lake.

She did an impression of us and even Veronica, one of the older girls who is usually serious and quite snooty, laughed. I don't think I've ever seen Veronica laugh like that before – usually it's when something bad happens to someone else.

At the end of class, Miss Marion called us to the front of the studio.

'I've got some news . . .' she began.

Rose looked at me. I'd told her I thought something was going on.

'The Grand Theatre is very honoured to announce that Mitzi Morgan has created a brand new ballet for us,' Miss Marion explained.

We all gasped. Mitzi Morgan was a famous choreographer. I'd heard Mum and Dad talking about her loads of times.

'But the extra-specially exciting thing about Mitzi's ballet is that it includes parts for children. And they're going to be played by some of you!' Miss Marion smiled.

Us? The studio erupted as we all started chattering excitedly.

'Shh! Shh, boys and girls!' Miss Marion laughed. 'Now, sadly, there aren't enough parts for everyone . . . so we're going to have an audition for Mitzi to choose the students she thinks are most suitable.'

An audition! The only audition Rose and I had ever done was when we'd auditioned for Extras last year.

'It will be held next Saturday during class,' Miss Marion explained, 'and it will be just like doing a normal class except Mitzi will be watching. To make sure everything's fair, you'll all be wearing numbers and I'll refer to you by your number only – no names.'

'Please, Miss Marion!' It was Veronica

with her hand up. 'How will we know what numbers we are?'

'I've got a list here,' Miss Marion said. 'I'll put it up in the changing room.'

Soon, we were crowding around the notice board. Veronica, with a smug smile on her face, turned to us and said, 'I'm number one! Rose is number nine. And you, Tilly, are thirteen. Imagine that? Fancy being stuck with thirteen!'

As Veronica moved to the other side of the changing room, I turned to Rose.

'What does she mean?' I asked. 'What's wrong with being thirteen?'

Rose shrugged. 'No idea.'

'You don't know?' Veronica sneered as she removed her shoes. 'You mean you've never heard of unlucky thirteen?'

'Thirteen is unlucky?' I gulped.

'Of course it isn't,' said Karina, coming over and giving me a hug.

Karina is fairly new to Extras. She's one of the older girls and really nice. She's really good at ballet too. Karina knows that sometimes Veronica can be a bit mean.

'Tell you what,' she said, 'my number is fourteen. Why don't we swap? I don't mind being thirteen.'

Veronica glared at her. She doesn't like it when Karina is friendly with us. Actually, she doesn't like it when *anyone* is friendly with us.

I smiled at Karina. 'Thanks, but it's OK. I'm happy with being thirteen.'

But after what Veronica had said, I wasn't sure it was true . . .

Chapter Two

After class, I headed off to the ballet wardrobe, like I usually did. Jessie, my godmother, was sitting at her huge worktable, busy stitching a costume.

'You'll never guess what's happening next week!' I gasped and told Jessie Miss Marion's news.

'I heard about the new ballet yesterday,' said Jessie. 'Isn't it exciting? So how are they going to choose who will play the children's parts?'

'There's going to be an audition in our Extras class next week,' I explained. 'Mitzi Morgan is coming to watch us dance.'

'Fantastic,' said Jessie. 'You're a super dancer. Just do your best and you'll be fine.'

'Will I?' I sighed. 'I've been given thirteen as my audition number.'

'What's wrong with being thirteen?' Jessie asked.

'Veronica says it's unlucky . . .'

'Nonsense.' Jessie shook her head and raised her eyes to the ceiling. 'It's the dancer who has the talent. How can the number you wear make you better or worse?'

And, as if she was agreeing with Jessie, Giselle leapt onto the table and said, 'Miaowwwww!'

I laughed. Giselle is the theatre cat, who made herself at home there last year. She's gorgeous and white and very nosy.

'So you think I'll be OK being thirteen?' I asked, stroking Giselle's ear as she jumped down and settled on my lap.

'I *know* you will,' said Jessie. 'And I also know a little bit about the ballet. Do you?'

I shook my head.

'Well I was told that the ballet is short – just one act,' said Jessie, 'and it's set in a park. All the characters are people who are visiting the park.'

'So that's why it needs children!' I said.

'Exactly,' said Jessie. 'The first sketches for the costumes have arrived – look.'

Jessie took a folder from the cupboard. There were all sorts of characters in amazing costumes. Some outfits were striped and others looked like they might be shimmery. The colours were bright and bold. I'd never seen ballet costumes like them before.

'They're incredible,' I said, really hoping I would be lucky enough to wear one.

Jessie was just putting the designs away when the big red doors of the ballet wardrobe opened.

'Mum! Dad!' I rushed over to give them a hug. 'You never told me there was going to be a new ballet!'

'We only found out about it today,' Dad explained.

'Have you heard there are going to be parts for children?' I asked. 'We're auditioning for them in Extras next week!'

Mum smiled and nodded. 'Isn't it exciting? But now we'd better get home for lunch. We can talk about it then!'

I said goodbye to Jessie and Giselle, and then and off we set. I couldn't wait to get home to find out even more about Mitzi and her new ballet.

Chapter Three

Myrtha was waiting for us in the hall. Myrtha is one of Giselle's kittens and she's gorgeous. I scooped her up in my arms and sat with her in the kitchen as Mum and Dad made lunch.

'Have you met Mitzi Morgan?' I asked.

'Once,' Mum said. 'She came to see us rehearsing last year. I think she must have come to take a look when she was thinking about her new ballet.'

'I saw a DVD of her dancing,' Dad

added. 'She was very athletic – really impressive!'

'Mitzi's ballet is going to be very different from the shows we usually do,' Mum said.

'Are you going to be in it?' I wondered.

'Yes,' said Dad, putting a bowl of salad on the kitchen table and then scooping his hand into mine he waltzed me up the hall.

'I love working on new ballets – and this one's going to be a world premiere!'

Dad twirled me around and danced us back down the hall to the kitchen where, with a small bow, he pulled out a chair for me to sit on.

'What will happen at the audition?' I wondered.

'Mitzi won't take the class,' Mum said, sitting down with me and Dad. 'She'll sit watching you – probably with the artistic director of the Grand Ballet.'

'We've got to wear numbers,' I added. 'I've got to wear thirteen!'

'Don't worry about that. I was thirteen once,' Mum said. 'I still got the part!'

'The number you wear makes no difference,' Dad agreed. 'Whenever you audition, you have to remember it's your dancing that they're looking at.'

'But sometimes they're looking for a certain type of dancer,' Mum warned.

'What do you mean?' I wondered. Surely if you were good, you were good?

'Well, they might be looking for a classical dancer,' said Mum. 'Or one that is better at being a comic character.'

'Yes,' added Dad. 'Or perhaps they might need a contemporary dancer. I once went for an audition not knowing they wanted a tap dancer. I was the only one there who couldn't tap. I felt really stupid!'

Dad pulled a sad, clown face and made us laugh.

Mum smiled. 'Everyone in Extras is in the same position. Some of you will be right for the parts Mitzi is looking for, others won't. Just do your best and enjoy it!'

I was starting to feel butterflies in my tummy already. The audition was scary.

But it was exciting at the same time. After all, how many children got the chance to try for a part in a world premiere at the Grand Theatre?

As well as ballet, I'm also learning the piano. Dad is a brilliant piano player so when he's at home he often plays with me. That afternoon, Dad asked if he could hear the new tune I was practising.

It was a jazzy piece about a clock, and the way the notes sounded was just like a clock ticking and then chiming midnight. I loved playing it and I jiggled on the piano stool in time with the music.

'That's really good, Tilly,' Dad said, pulling up his own chair next to me. 'Let's see if we can turn it into a duet. On the count of three, you start at the beginning.'

We had great fun, with Dad playing dramatic notes at the bottom of the keyboard and then standing up, whizzing round me and playing tinkly high notes at the other end! And Myrtha seemed to like it too. She sat watching us from the sofa as we played. Then she jumped onto the arm of the nearest chair, twitching her head to each side in time with the tune. Suddenly, Myrtha leapt from the chair and landed on the keyboard.

Clink, tinkle, plonk! Her paws clattered along the keys.

'Miaow!' she announced.

And we both laughed.

On Sunday, Rose came round to play. I told her what Mum and Dad had said about auditions.

'I wonder if Veronica is working out how she can be in the front row?' Rose joked.

Veronica was always trying to make sure she was right in front of Miss Marion in class. She'd be desperate to be seen by an important choreographer.

I giggled and stuck the straw in my carton of juice.

'Oh yuck!' I yelped.

I'd squirted juice all down my top and it was trickling down my leg.

'Quick,' said Rose, trying to wipe it up. 'Before it goes on your sparkly trainers.'

'Bad luck, Tilly,' said Mum, coming in and helping me clean up the mess.

'Thanks,' I sighed, taking off my T-shirt.

Bad luck. That's what Veronica had said about being number thirteen. Maybe she was right after all . . .

Chapter Four

On Tuesday after school, Rose's mum Helen takes us to another ballet class at Miss Nancy's. Miss Nancy was my mum's teacher when she was little.

That afternoon, we'd already left the playground when I realised I'd left my ballet bag at school so I had to rush back to fetch it. Then, when we arrived at Miss Nancy's studio and I'd changed into my leotard I discovered I only had one shoe in my bag.

'It must be there,' said Rose, helping me look again.

It wasn't.

'I can't dance with one shoe!' I sighed.

And now it was time for our class to begin.

'Lots of people forget their shoes,' Miss Nancy smiled when I explained. 'Let's see what I've got in my cupboard . . . Here! Try these.'

She pulled out a black pair of ballet shoes. They were quite different from the pink satin ones that Mum had bought me for my ballet exam last term, but at least they fitted.

'Thanks, Miss Nancy,' I said.

Phew! That was lucky. If she hadn't found some shoes, I wouldn't have been able to dance. And I needed all the practice I could get before the audition.

'Now then, girls,' Miss Nancy said. 'Let's take our places at the *barre*.'

We were learning new steps for the next grade and another ballet exam. It felt really grown up to be doing the more difficult work. Miss Nancy said everything we were learning was to prepare us for when we were older and needed to have strong feet and legs to do *pointe* work in special *pointe* shoes!

In the centre, we concentrated on some of the *retirés* exercises that we were learning, as well as new head and feet placements. One day, we would be ready to pirouette without tripping over or getting dizzy!

After class, we couldn't wait to tell Miss Nancy about the audition.

'A new ballet from Mitzi Morgan!' Miss

Nancy exclaimed. 'And fancy you getting the chance to audition for it!'

'We're really excited!' said Rose.

'And really scared!' I added.

'Being a bit of both is exactly what will make you dance your best,' Miss Nancy said. 'Just enjoy it. Mitzi won't want to see miserable dancers, will she?'

We shook our heads and hoped we would be confident enough to smile like she suggested.

'Good luck,' Miss Nancy said, giving us both a hug. 'And don't forget to tell me all about it!'

Later that night, I was tucked up in bed, reading. As usual, Myrtha was curled up on my toes. I got to the end of the chapter and put the book on the floor. Next to it was my ballet tin.

It had been given to me by Jessie and was really special. Special for lots of reasons. Firstly, it was given to me by Jessie. Secondly, it had a picture of the ballet *Giselle* on the lid. Jessie had given it to me when the Grand Ballet had performed *Giselle*, which was when Giselle the cat had arrived at the theatre too. I keep all the special ballet souvenirs I've collected in it. Souvenirs like a photo of me presenting flowers to Madame Satina, the founder of the Grand Ballet, at a special gala show. And glittery beads and sequins from some of the ballerinas' costumes.

I picked up the tin and opened it, stroking the shiny beads and sequins. *Would I ever get to wear a ballet costume with beautiful things like these on it?* I wondered. I closed the lid and, just before I turned off the light, I glanced at the poster on my wall. It's something Dad gave me and is just like one of the real posters they have up outside the Grand Theatre. Only this one has me as the ballerina and says 'Starring Chantilly Tippington' underneath. It's amazing.

I switched off the light and shut my eyes, but I couldn't sleep. I thought about how silly I'd been not to check that both shoes were in my ballet bag. I'd found the missing shoe on the floor of my bedroom when I got home . . . What if I forgot my ballet shoes at the audition on Saturday? My chance to get on stage would be over before it had even begun!

Chapter Five

'Oh my goodness, Tilly! What on Earth have you done?' Jessie asked as I turned up at the ballet wardrobe on Wednesday afternoon. 'There's blood pouring down your socks!'

'Quick – sit down!' Adam said, lifting me up onto a stool. Adam works in the ballet wardrobe with Jessie, making costumes.

I was trying hard not to cry because my knee really hurt.

'What happened?' Jessie wanted to

know as she and Adam opened the first-aid kit and started to wipe my knee.

'Ouch!' I hissed. The antiseptic wipe stung. 'I was getting off the bus just now and I tripped ...'

'Bad luck, Tilly,' Adam said. 'Here – how about I give you this beautiful blue plaster?'

For a plaster, it was quite cool. But Adam had said those words again – *bad luck*.

'Everything keeps going wrong!' I sobbed. 'Ever since I got given number thirteen!'

Giselle came over to wrap herself round my legs and purred as if to say she was sorry about my leg too.

'What's gone wrong?' said Jessie, giving me a hug.

I told her about spilling my drink and forgetting my ballet shoe – and now cutting my knee.

'How can I do an audition with a great big plaster on my knee?' I wailed.

'No one will see it,' Jessie pointed out.

'No,' agreed Adam. 'Not under a pair of ballet tights!'

Of course!

'I think you need a treat,' said Jessie. 'How about we go to the canteen and see what we can find?'

I smiled. That sounded like a good idea.

'Come on,' Jessie helped me down from the stool. 'Let's go!'

We left Giselle curled up in her basket in the ballet wardrobe and set off down the corridor.

We could hear music coming from the orchestra's rehearsal room. The tune was bright and light and made me want to skip and gallop.

'That's beautiful, isn't it?' I said.

'I think it's the music for the new ballet,' said Jessie.

She waved her arms at her sides in time with the rhythm. I joined in and we did a little polka towards the canteen.

'Ouch!' I said, touching my knee. It really hurt!

'Don't worry,' Jessie said, opening the door of the canteen. 'The bruising will have gone down by tomorrow. Now – let's get you that treat!'

Jessie was right! My knee felt much better the next day. Mum took me to school and we picked up Rose on the way.

On the bus, I told Rose about the music I'd heard the day before.

'I wonder if they'll play it at the audition?' she wondered.

'That would be brilliant,' I agreed.

'Better put your macs on, girls,' Mum suggested as we got closer to school. 'It's raining quite hard now.'

When the bus stopped, Rose and I hopped off and pulled up our hoods.

'Look out!' Mum warned.

'Look out for . . . ? Oh!'

Splosh! Before I could finish my question, I stepped in the biggest puddle you can imagine. And then the other foot went splashing into the water. Both my feet were soaked.

'Bad luck, Tilly,' Rose said, offering me her hand to help me wade out.

'How come you didn't get wet?' I asked.

Rose shrugged her shoulders. 'I just saw it.'

'Never mind,' Mum said. 'You can wear your plimsolls until your school shoes are dry. Come on – we'd better get into school before we *all* get wet.'

I felt cross and grumpy. Why did bad things keep happening to *me*?

Chapter Six

I tried to forget about everything. But on Friday I managed to lose my pencil case. I was sure it had been in my school bag, but I couldn't find it anywhere. Our teacher said it would probably turn up when everyone went home and that she'd keep it for me, ready for Monday.

But that didn't make things any better. I was fed up with all my bad luck. I told Mum and Dad how I felt when they came to collect me from school.

'Stick with me, Tilly,' said Dad, giving me a hug. 'I'm having a lucky afternoon. After all, I don't have a rehearsal or a performance so I've been able to come and meet you – isn't that great?'

I grinned. It really was extra special having him *and* Mum fetch me from school. Because of their work, it hardly ever happened. I looked up at him and smiled.

'It's absolutely brilliant,' I agreed.

We made the most of our time and went straight to *Dance! Dance!* which sells all kinds of beautiful dance shoes and clothes and is my absolutely most favourite shop in the world. Mum and Dad bought me a new pair of ballet tights so I would look smart for my audition.

'I know Mitzi won't be looking at your

clothes,' Mum said. 'But if you feel good, I always think it makes you dance better.'

When we got home, Dad helped me with my homework, so it would be out of the way for the weekend. We sat on the sofa with Myrtha, learning spellings.

'I'm impressed!' Dad said when I got them all right.

'So am I,' Mum added, stroking Myrtha. 'Now, shall we go upstairs and get everything ready for tomorrow?'

'Yes, please!' I nodded. With my record of losing and forgetting things, I didn't want to leave anything to chance.

'Let's lay everything out on the bed so we can see what we've got,' Mum suggested.

Ballet shoes, leotard, new tights, crossover, hair stuff – it was all there, folded neatly.

'Miaowww!'

Myrtha jumped up on top of everything.

'Hey, puss!' I said, gently lifting her up. 'I'm going to have to move you – we don't want your claws snagging my new tights!'

Myrtha smooched her face into my neck.

'We certainly don't,' Mum giggled. 'Now, I think we should include some just-in-case stuff.'

'What's just-in-case stuff?' I asked.

'Just in case you get a ladder or something,' Mum said.

'A ladder in my new tights?' I queried.

I put my hand down and stroked them through the packet. They felt smooth and silky. Ballet tights are much thicker than the kind of tights Mum wears. I couldn't think how they could get laddered.

'You might catch them on the bench in the changing room,' Mum suggested. 'Or snag them on the door.'

I shivered at the thought. Mum was right about what she'd said earlier – you felt great if you looked smart. When Jessie had made me a beautiful dress to wear at the gala show, I'd felt like a princess. And I wanted to dance like one too.

'So should we take my spare leotard?' I asked.

Mum nodded. 'Two leotards, two pairs of tights – and just the one crossover. You won't need to wear it once you're in the studio.'

'But what about my shoes?' I wondered. 'I want to wear the satin ones I wore for my ballet exam.'

'Perfect,' Mum said. 'But we'll take your old leather ones, too – just in case! And I'll get all your hair stuff ready for the morning.'

Carefully, we placed everything into my ballet bag and put it in the hall.

'Quick, you two!' Dad called out. 'Come and watch this – Mitzi Morgan's on the local news. She's talking about the new ballet!'

Mitzi Morgan was on the telly? This I had to see!

Chapter Seven

The next morning, I didn't really feel like eating breakfast. I'd seen what a brilliant dancer Mitzi Morgan had been on the telly last night. Now I was scared. She was going to expect us all to be amazing too. But Dad said no dancer can work on an empty stomach. So we all ate together.

As soon as I'd cleaned my teeth, I couldn't keep still. I kept looking at the clock – I didn't want to be late.

'Let's fix your hair now,' Mum said.

'Shall we do a plait or a bun?'

'A bun, please!'

So I sat on a kitchen stool while Mum did my hair. She was so quick, you could tell that she'd done it a million times before!

'How does that feel?' Mum asked, patting the bun at the back. 'Secure?'

I waggled my head. The bun didn't move.

'It's fine,' I said.

'Come on then,' Mum smiled. 'I think we'd all feel happier if we set off now!'

At the theatre, Dad wished me luck and went off to a class but Mum came with me to the changing room. The place was packed. Rose and her mum were already there. In fact, everyone's mum had come to help get them ready and wish them luck.

I pulled on my leotard and tights and Mum tied up my ballet shoes. When Rose and I were dressed, we did a twirl to check everything was OK and then hugged each other. We were ready for the audition!

'Oh no!' A scream came from the other side of the room. It was Veronica.

'What's up?' Karina asked.

'My shoe ribbon is loose!' Veronica wailed.

'I haven't got any sewing thread!' Veronica's mum panicked.

'Leave it to me,' said Mum, diving into her huge ballet bag. 'Here – a sewing kit!'

Mum always carried everything – and more – that a dancer could need. Veronica's mum was gushing with her thanks but Veronica had to be pushed over to say thank you. It was like she was cross my mum had helped her out. Oh well – that was *her* problem!

'Shall I hand out the audition numbers?' Karina suggested.

She handed me my thirteen. I gulped as Mum pinned it to my front. Thirteen . . .

'Forget all that nonsense,' she popped a kiss on my cheek. 'You'll be fine!'

I smiled. It felt good to have Mum there in the changing room, helping me get ready. That *had* to be good luck!

'Someone's missing . . .' Karina said, holding up the last number. 'Where's Hayley?'

There were only ten minutes to go before the audition was due to start. Hayley was going to be late!

'Come on, girls,' Mum suggested. 'I think you should make your way to the studio. After all, if Hayley is cutting it fine, she'll need more space to get ready quickly.'

Mum and Rose's mum, Helen, wished us luck and then we set off. We were walking along the corridor when Bob, who sits by the Stage Door, stopped us.

'Hello, girls,' he smiled. 'Are you going to see Miss Marion?'

We nodded.

'Then I wonder if one of you could give her this note?' Bob asked.

'If that's for Miss Marion it will be

important,' said Veronica. She snatched the note from Bob's hand and raced towards the studio. 'So I'd better make sure she gets it!'

I pulled a face. Why did Veronica always think she was in charge?

'Come on,' shrugged Karina. 'We'd better get going.'

We trooped off behind her.

'But where,' I wondered, 'is Hayley? If she doesn't turn up soon, she'll miss the audition!'

Chapter Eight

By the time we got to the studio, the boys were already waiting, and Veronica had barged her way in.

Miss Marion appeared at the door.

'Ready, everyone? Come on then – let's start.'

Veronica had bagged the best place at the *barre*, as usual. The rest of us filled in the gaps where Miss Marion told us to stand. I rested my hand on the *barre* and faced the front of the studio. In the middle of the mirror that covered the front wall, I could see the man I knew was the artistic director of the Grand Ballet. He was sitting on a chair next to a woman.

'Morning, everyone,' Miss Marion announced. 'I'd like to introduce Mitzi Morgan, who is choreographing a wonderful new ballet for us.'

'Hello,' Mitzi smiled. 'It's great to be here – I'm really looking forward to seeing you dance!'

She seemed nice. Maybe this wouldn't be quite so scary after all? Miss Marion turned back to the class.

'Sadly, I've had a message to say that Hayley's ill and won't be able to join us today,' she said.

We gasped. So *that* was what Bob's note had said. Hayley was one of the older girls at Extras and she was a really good dancer. She'd be devastated to miss this opportunity. I looked at Rose, who was standing at the *barre* behind me.

'Poor Hayley,' she whispered.

'Now,' Miss Marion said. '*Pliés!*'

The audition had begun.

If you could forget that every move you made was being watched and you had a number stuck on your front, it was just like doing class. At first, I couldn't stop looking at Mitzi and the artistic director.

Who were they watching? What were they whispering to each other? I wondered.

But then I realised I was being silly. They were meant to be watching *me* – not me watching *them*! I should be concentrating on my dancing. So, as the music continued, I tried harder to think about what Miss

Marion was saying. Soon, I was lost in my *retirés*, *degagés* and *grand battement*.

When we moved to do our centre work, Miss Marion kept us in the same lines of dancers that she always did. And as usual we changed which line was in front so we all got a turn to be seen clearly by Mitzi.

I could see the director pointing at some of us and then chatting to Mitzi as we danced. It was so much harder to pretend they weren't there in the centre!

We were about halfway through our centre work when Miss Marion announced that the next routine would be taught to us by Mitzi.

'I'll just show you from the front – music, please!' Mitzi grinned.

She stood facing us and then went through an *enchainment* of steps. She made it look like fun.

'So, shall we mark that through together?'

We nodded. I couldn't wait to join in! Mitzi turned her back on us and glanced behind her as she marked the steps of the *enchainment* slowly. Then she went back to her seat and the music started up again.

We did it each line in turn and then got a chance to do it a second time as well. It was amazing. I loved the music and it just made me want to dance. I was smiling as I danced it through again.

Then Mitzi decided we should do another *enchainment*. As before, she showed us the steps. This time, it started over at the top corner of the studio, as if we were entering from the wings of a stage. When she was sure we knew the steps, Miss Marion suggested that mine and Rose's line went first.

We stood at the corner, our right feet pointed behind us, ready to go. It was crowded at the back of the line, and I could feel someone right behind me. One, two three . . . two, two, three . . . we counted ourselves in and then off we . . . CRASH!

I hadn't even managed to get beyond the first beat and I'd fallen flat on my face!

Chapter Nine

It was so embarrassing! The music stopped and everyone was staring at me. My big toe hurt. I must have stubbed it before I fell. And my face was covered in gritty rosin from people's shoes. My knee – the same knee that I'd cut the other day – was killing me. But what had I tripped on? Had it been the person behind who was so close to me?

Miss Marion, Rose, Karina and some others rushed over to help me get up.

'I tripped on something . . . Sorry . . .' I said, my cheeks flushing pink then red.

The whole audition had come to a stop because of me. I felt so stupid.

'Sit down and get your breath back,' Miss Marion smiled. 'Then you can join in again.'

Rose helped me to the back of the studio along with some of the other girls. Karina was going to come with me too but Miss Marion suggested that her line did the routine first.

I looked up and saw that Veronica was in that line too. And Veronica was standing where I had been before I fell over. In *exactly* the same place. I could see her nasty smile in the studio mirror. She was looking very pleased with herself.

'Veronica was ever so close to you before you fell,' Rose whispered to me before she rejoined the group. 'I wondered if you'd lost your balance because of the crush.'

Hmmm. I was sure that I had tripped over something. And now I was wondering if it was Veronica's foot . . . My knee was sore. I rubbed it – it was wet! My knee had started to bleed again! I could feel tears welling up in my eyes. The audition had started so well. Now it was a disaster and everything was going wrong.

I wiped my tears and covered my knee with my hand. From the back of the studio, everyone else was looking good. Veronica and Karina's line had finished and now Rose, in the line I should have been, was dancing. Rose was doing the steps perfectly. How I wished I were too!

Karina came up to me. 'Are you OK?' she whispered.

I nodded – but I didn't feel OK.

'Let's do that one more time, boys and girls,' Miss Marion said as the last line was finishing.

Karina took her place in line again and then they were off. Rose and the others gathered at the back, ready for their turn. There was no way I was going to miss another go. Quickly, I joined the line. Seconds later, I was dancing. I was determined to show Mitzi what I could do.

I smiled and danced my heart out to the music. I could feel Mitzi and the director looking at me. Was it because I'd made a mess of my entry before? And then the music stopped and it was over. Miss Marion gave me a quick wink as if to say 'well done' and then we were all told to go back to our lines. We did our *reverence* to Mitzi and the director, who clapped.

'I've really enjoyed watching everyone this morning,' Mitzi grinned. 'What a talented group of young dancers you are!'

Her smile was so infectious it was impossible not to smile back, even with a sore knee. Then we made our way back to the changing room.

'Are you OK?' Rose asked, hugging me as soon as we got out of the studio.

'I think so,' I nodded. But inside I felt small and stupid.

'Well you made a right show of yourself today, didn't you?' Veronica hissed.

'Tilly didn't do it on purpose!' Karina stepped in, before I could say anything.

'Tilly! Rose!' a voice called behind us. It was Mum. 'How did it go?'

I looked at Mum, feeling like I'd let her and Dad down. Then I burst into tears.

Chapter Ten

'Come on,' Mum said, scooping me gently into the changing room, where all the mums were waiting. 'Tell me what's wrong.'

Mum handed me a tissue and Rose explained about me falling over and my knee bleeding.

'Never mind, love,' Mum soothed, 'these things happen. But I'm impressed you didn't let it stop you from dancing.'

I nodded. Veronica was glaring at me, completely ignoring her own mum.

Suddenly, the door opened and Miss Marion entered. She came over and asked me how I was.

'Fine thanks,' I sighed.

'She'll be OK,' Mum smiled.

'Well, girls,' Miss Marion said, turning to all the Extras in the changing room. 'I was extremely pleased with your performance today. Mitzi and our artistic director both said how impressed they were. And Mitzi has made her choice already . . .'

Rose and I looked at each other. I felt wretched. I knew I'd ruined my chance… My chance of being in the world premiere of Mitzi's ballet!

'Please remember that the girls who've been chosen aren't necessarily better dancers,' Miss Marion explained. 'It's because they fit into the roles that Mitzi has choreographed.'

The room was deadly silent as everyone listened eagerly.

'So, the girls that Mitzi would like to use are . . .'

Miss Marion began to call them out. Veronica was chosen. So was Karina. And Rose! I squeezed Rose's hand – that was fantastic. I smiled at the other girls as they grinned when their numbers were called.

'Well done!' Mum clapped.

Who was she talking to?

'Yes – well done!' Helen said.

I looked at them, puzzled.

'You made it, Tilly!' Rose grinned.

Me? And then I realised – I'd been so convinced I wouldn't be picked, I hadn't even heard Miss Marion call out thirteen! I'd been given a part in the ballet too!

I changed and raced to the ballet wardrobe with Mum following.

'Jessie, Jessie!' I screamed, bursting through the red doors. 'You'll never guess what!'

'I think I might,' Jessie smiled, getting up to greet me.

'I've only gone and got a part in the new ballet! Even though I fell over and everything. And so has Rose! And Karina! There's ten girls who have been given parts.

And some boys – but I don't know who they are yet.'

'That's wonderful news,' Jessie said, kissing the top of my head. 'Well done to you all. But what's all this about falling over . . . ? Sit down and tell me everything.'

So I repeated the whole story. Adam and Belinda were in the ballet wardrobe and they stopped their sewing and came to listen too.

'You poor thing,' Belinda sighed.

'But you were brave to carry on,' Adam said.

'Just like a real dancer,' Jessie announced.

Mum nodded. 'I'm so proud of you!'

And as if to say she was too, Giselle jumped up onto Jessie's worktable and skipped across it, scooping a reel of cotton along with her paws. She looked just like she was dancing and we all laughed.

'Funny to think you're going to be dancing on stage with your mum and dad,' Jessie grinned.

'Dad!' I yelped. 'When can I tell him?'

Mum looked at her watch. 'He should be finished by now. Shall we go down and meet him at the Stage Door?'

'Good idea,' Jessie declared. 'And I tell you what – why don't we all go out for a celebratory tea?'

'Thanks,' I smiled. This was turning out to be one of the best days ever!

Chapter Eleven

When Rose and I told Miss Nancy the news on Tuesday, she started clapping.

'I'll have to find out when the performances are,' she said. 'I don't want to miss seeing two of my dancers on stage at the Grand Theatre!'

On stage at the Grand Theatre ... It sounded so grown up.

'I'm not sure when opening night is but the first rehearsal's on Thursday,' Rose explained.

'Excellent,' Miss Nancy grinned. 'I can't wait to hear more!'

On Thursday, all the Extras who had parts gathered in the studio with Miss Marion.

'The ballet is called *Promenade*,' she explained, 'and it takes place in a park. You're going to play children who are there with their family and friends. Now, the first performance is in two months' time and there's lots to do, so let's start learning some steps.'

The pianist began to play and we watched Miss Marion closely as she marked out the steps. I'd had trouble learning dances before, but the music for this ballet was so catchy and the steps so much fun that it didn't seem so difficult this time.

The rehearsal was an hour and a half —

much longer than our usual class, but we were working so hard that the time went by in a flash.

'Wasn't that amazing?' Karina declared in the changing room afterwards.

'I loved every minute,' said Rose, skipping around the room.

'Me too!' everyone agreed and then laughed because we realised we'd all spoken at the same time.

Everyone except for Veronica who, now that she was in the ballet, seemed to think she was even more important than ever.

'You are all such babies,' she sniffed, poking her nose into the air. 'Dancers don't behave like idiots.'

But that only made us laugh more.

'What's wrong with having some fun?' I said. 'Mum and Dad are always laughing about stuff that happens at work.'

Veronica glared at me. 'You're always going on about your famous mum and dad. You get special treatment because of them.'

'What?' I couldn't believe what I was hearing.

'Just ignore her,' Rose whispered.

So I did. But it made me wonder. *Were other people thinking the same thing?*

I asked Jessie about it afterwards.

'Don't be daft! Mitzi chose you – and the others – because you're good dancers and you fitted the roles.'

I hoped what she said was true, but I couldn't help thinking about the mistake I'd made. Did I really deserve the part?

'So what did you do in rehearsal?' Jessie asked, changing the subject.

I showed Jessie the steps we'd been learning.

'Let me try!' she said and skipped around the worktable.

Jessie sort of got the steps but she was very wobbly. Giselle looked up and then gave a great big yawn and then settled back to sleep.

'I don't think she's very impressed,' giggled Adam who was watching us from his sewing machine. 'You're not nearly as good as Tilly!'

He winked at me. I felt better already.

'No,' Jessie smiled. 'I'd better stick to my stitching! Oh, look at the time!'

'Have you forgotten something?' I wondered.

'Well Alfie in the scenery department mentioned they were starting on the scenery for the ballet this morning,' Jessie explained. 'So I thought we'd go and see what they're doing.'

The scenery department is amazing. Like a huge, tall warehouse full of enormous painted panels that are stored for every ballet.

One area has the workshop where they paint new stuff. Each piece of scenery is called a flat. Flats are gigantic pieces of canvas on huge timber frames. Just like enormous paintings.

'Hello, Tilly!' Alfie said when he saw us. 'Have you come to see the new scenery?'

I nodded. 'Do you have some designs to work from?'

'Here, take a look at these,' Alfie said, showing us some sheets of paper.

You could see scenes that looked just

like a park, with swings and a pond and even birds flying through the sky.

'I wish I could paint as well as that,' I sighed.

'Well I wish I could dance as well as you!' Alfie said, and then he made an attempt at a pirouette. 'But as you see I can't! So it's a good job I can make scenery instead.'

Jessie and I giggled. Alfie's dancing was just like Jessie's.

'Come on,' said Jessie. 'Time for a cup of tea.'

'Excellent,' said Alfie. 'Make one for me and I'll see you in a minute!'

We'd just set off down the corridor when I heard someone calling my name. It was Mia and Gus! They'd just come out of a rehearsal too. Mia and Gus were some of the youngest dancers in the Grand Ballet. It wasn't so long ago that they were dancers in Extras.

'We heard that you and Rose have parts in the new ballet,' Gus said.

'Yes,' I smiled. 'Are you in it too?'

They nodded.

'Isn't it great to be working with Mitzi Morgan,' Mia announced. 'Maybe we'll be in some scenes together!'

'I think we are,' said Gus. 'You're coming to rehearsal on Saturday, aren't you?'

I nodded.

'There's not long until our first performance,' I said. 'Do you think we'll learn everything in time?'

'Of course,' said Mia. 'But it's going to be hard work!'

Chapter Twelve

Mitzi was at the first full rehearsal on Saturday. At the start I felt nervous around her but she soon made us feel relaxed and we couldn't wait to start practising.

Mitzi took each group through their routines and when we weren't dancing, we sat and watched. You learn so much from seeing other dancers working.

Rose and I were playing sisters and we were introduced to Charlie and Cynthia, the dancers who were playing our parents.

I'd met them before with my parents and they're really nice. In the ballet though, Rose and I were meant to drive them mad with our bad behaviour and then look upset when they told us off!

Because they were among the tallest, Karina and Veronica were in a group of older girls who were on a school trip with their teacher, played by Mia! And Gus was playing a boy on a bicycle who wanted to ask Mia out.

Some of the boys from Extras were boys who hid behind bushes and flicked things at the schoolgirls, another boy was playing a son out with his dad. Mitzi said he was going to have to climb on the dancer's shoulders to get a cat out of a tree for a dancer who was pretending to be an elderly lady. I wondered if Giselle would get a role too!

The rehearsal lasted the whole afternoon and when it finally ended I was starving. And exhausted too. As we got ready to leave, Miss Marion, who had also been with us, explained that in some rehearsals we would be split up, so each group of us could concentrate on their own storylines, but every Saturday, just like today, we'd all practise together.

'But we need everyone here again on Tuesday too,' she went on, 'for your first costume fitting – don't forget!'

Forget? Rose and I grinned at each other. We couldn't wait!

So the next Tuesday, instead of going to Miss Nancy's, Helen took me and Rose to the ballet wardrobe. It was quite crowded inside with all the other Extras. As usual,

Veronica seemed to think that she was in charge and introduced us all to Jessie.

'Oh I already know Tilly and Rose,' Jessie said.

Veronica glared at us but I just smiled back, which made her temper worse.

Jessie showed us the costume designer's drawings of each of our characters.

'They're gorgeous!' Karina sighed and everyone agreed.

Our costumes were kind of mad. But nice mad. Like we were part of a fairy-tale world. Rose and I were wearing big puffy-out skirts and crazy, stripy tights with purple ballet shoes. They were not the sort of clothes you'd wear normally, but they made great costumes – like brightly wrapped sweets!

Our hair was going to be in plaits that curled out at the sides. Jessie told us they'd do that with wiry things, which would be plaited into our hair!

Adam, Belinda and Jessie divided us into three groups and took our measurements, which were carefully marked down in Jessie's notebook.

As the last of us were being measured, Miss Marion arrived in the wardrobe.

'Is everything OK?' she asked, smiling.

We nodded.

'Excellent,' Miss Marion said. 'I can't wait to see you in your costumes.'

'Nor can we!' exclaimed Karina, speaking for all of us.

Over the next five weeks, Rose and I got into a routine of having class with Miss Nancy on Tuesday, then rehearsal with Charlie and Cynthia on Thursday, and Extras on Saturday followed by a full cast rehearsal. It was incredible how much we learned in such a short time. And how brilliant it was to be part of it.

At the end of one Saturday rehearsal, with just under three weeks to go before the opening night, Miss Marion called the Extras over to her.

'I've got some news about the rehearsal next Thursday,' she said. 'A photographer's coming to take pictures – it's a photocall.'

'Please, miss,' Rose asked. 'What's a photocall?'

'It's for the press,' Veronica said, like some super-smart teacher. 'The photos will be sent to newspapers to get publicity for the ballet.'

There was a gasp of excitement. Could being in this ballet get any better?

Doing all the rehearsals, classes and costume fittings was brilliant but I had no time – or energy – to do anything else. I think all the other Extras felt the same.

'We've learned so much in such a short time,' I said, stifling another yawn as I sat with Myrtha after my Tuesday class.

'There's lots to remember,' Dad agreed.

Myrtha purred as I stroked her. The rhythm made the ballet music leap into my head. I imagined myself dancing to it.

'Tilly?' Mum said, putting her hand on my shoulder. 'Tilly?'

I jumped, lost in my daydream.

'Come on,' Mum laughed. 'Let's go and get your homework finished before supper. I think it might be an early night for you!'

Myrtha always likes to go outside and explore our garden after supper. Tonight, I noticed, she was gone for longer than usual and she wasn't back when I went up for my bath. I knew I was getting ready for bed earlier than usual, but Myrtha still wasn't in when I was tucked up, listening to Dad reading to me.

'It's strange not to have Myrtha on my feet,' I said.

'She'll be back soon,' Dad said, closing the book and switching off my light. 'And as soon as she is, she'll be on her way up for a cuddle. Night night, sweetheart.'

He pecked me on my cheek and went downstairs. As I lay there, I thought I'd just run over my steps again in my head as I waited for Myrtha. But I was so tired, I didn't get much further than the first gallop . . .

Chapter Thirteen

In the morning, I was positively bursting with energy! I sprang out of bed, washed and dressed. Myrtha must have gone down for her breakfast already, I thought as I pulled on my school shoes and raced downstairs for mine.

'Where's Myrtha?' I asked Dad, who was cooking.

Dad sighed. 'Er, she still seems to be out . . .'

'You mean she didn't come in last night?'

That wasn't like Myrtha. She always spent the night on my bed! I opened the back door and called her for ages and ages. But she didn't appear.

In the end, Dad said, 'Why don't you come in for your breakfast? She's bound to come back for hers any minute.'

But she didn't. And she hadn't returned after school either. I stood in the garden and called and called. But she never came.

'What if she's hurt?' I sobbed to Mum.

'Oh, darling,' Mum hugged me.

'I bet she's curled up asleep somewhere warm,' Dad said. 'If she hasn't come back by tomorrow morning, we'll do some posters. We can put them up in the street.'

I wiped my nose.

'Thanks, Dad,'

'Don't worry, sweetheart,' he said. 'I'm sure we won't need to.'

It was dreadful spending another night without Myrtha. And there was still no sign of her next morning, even when I called her name.

'Come on,' said Dad. 'We've just got time to do something on the laptop before you go to school.'

I helped Dad paste a photo of Myrtha onto a document. We wrote MYRTHA IS MISSING on the top and PLEASE LET US KNOW IF YOU'VE SEEN HER on the bottom with our phone number. Then we stuck it to our front gate and some lampposts on our way to school.

I really hoped she'd be there when I got home . . .

After school, Rose's mum took us to the theatre. The photographer was there when we arrived. And so were some of the grown-ups who were in the ballet too.

Quick as a flash, the photographer took some shots of us as we gathered in the studio. Then she said she'd hang around after the rehearsal began.

Miss Marion told us to go through the linking routines. When we were on stage, these would show us walking round the park before a group of characters danced their story.

'Excellent!' Miss Marion called out as she mingled between us, suggesting we did things like look in a particular direction or pretend to chat to each other as we passed by. 'It's got to seem realistic, like a real walk in the park.'

As we danced, we forgot about the photographer. But every now and then she was suddenly there as you went towards her. She moved silently and swiftly amongst us, almost like a dancer herself.

The music stopped.

'Right,' announced Miss Marion. 'Let's take a breather. Everyone back in ten minutes, please!'

As we headed over to the studio door, the photographer came over and said, 'Can I just take your names, girls? I need to put some captions with the photos.'

So we told her and then she looked at me and said, 'Chantilly Tippington . . . I remember you from the gala show. Your parents are dancers here too, aren't they?'

I nodded.

'I thought I recognised you!' she said. 'It must be great having a mum and dad who both dance.'

'It is,' I agreed. 'Really special.'

'Excellent,' she said, scribbling things down in her notebook. 'Well, thanks, girls – I'll look forward to seeing you on stage!'

Veronica was already in the changing room, her arms crossed and her face crosser.

'There you go again!' she snapped as

she saw me. 'Always talking about your famous mum and dad.'

Before I could say anything, Rose said, 'That's not fair! Tilly didn't mention her mum and dad until the photographer asked her.'

'No, I didn't,' I declared.

'Everyone knows you only got a part in the ballet because of who they are,' Veronica hissed. 'You're a rubbish dancer!'

Then she stormed out of the room.

Chapter Fourteen

Mum and Dad appeared in the studio at the end of the rehearsal, ready to take me and Rose home. We dropped Rose off first and then I raced inside the house, desperate to see Myrtha curled up in her basket in the kitchen, as if she'd been there all day.

But it was empty. I looked at Mum and Dad. My bottom lip wobbled.

'Come on,' said Dad before I started to cry. 'Let's go and call for her in the garden.'

We must have called Myrtha's name

a hundred times but she didn't appear. I couldn't bear it!

'Let's put our coats on,' said Dad, 'and go and call for her down the street.'

We were at the front door when Mum rushed through from the kitchen.

'Wait!' she said. 'There's a message on the phone. A lady at number thirteen thinks she's found Myrtha locked in her garden shed!'

'Come on,' I said. 'Let's go!'

It *was* Myrtha!

'Miaoowwwww,' she went as soon as she saw me, and rushed over to us. I scooped her up in my arms and snuggled my face in her warm fur as she purred. I think Myrtha had missed me as much as I'd missed her.

'I was potting up some plants a couple of nights ago,' the lady explained. 'She must have sneaked inside without me noticing her. I'm so sorry! I locked the shed and went inside. I had no idea she was there until I came out this afternoon and heard her miaowing!'

'Thanks so much for finding her,' I said.

'I'm just sorry it happened,' the lady said. 'Next time I'll check the shed's empty before locking up.'

'Thanks,' said Dad. 'Now come on, Tilly, we'd better get Mytha back and give her some food.'

'Miaow!'

We all laughed.

'Sounds like she agrees,' I said. 'Thanks again.'

And with Myrtha clinging to me, we walked home.

'Funny to think that all that time she was only a couple of houses away,' Dad said, giving us both a hug.

At number thirteen, I thought, *where Myrtha had been safe, after all. Maybe thirteen wasn't so unlucky after all . . .*

Myrtha was starving! She almost knocked my hand away as I put down her food bowl. And when she'd finally finished eating, she purred as we all made a huge fuss of her.

'Thank goodness for that,' Mum said as we watched Myrtha run up the stairs.

'Well,' Dad smiled. 'I think we can guess where she's off to sleep now!'

Much later, I slipped under my duvet and Myrtha was still curled at the foot of my bed. She didn't open her eyes but I think she knew I was there because she twitched her ear and purred gently as I kissed her head.

'I can't believe how much I missed her,' I said to Mum when she came up to say goodnight.

'We all did,' agreed Mum. 'The house seemed so empty without her.'

Mum read a chapter of my book to me then we both stifled a yawn.

'Golly,' she said. 'I think we need an early night – it's all those rehearsals!'

'But I love it,' I sighed. 'It's amazing to see how everything in the ballet is coming together. How everyone has learned their parts and now we're putting it all in place. Like a jigsaw puzzle!'

Mum laughed. 'I suppose it is – and in a few weeks we'll be putting the costumes on and dancing with the orchestra instead of the piano.'

I hugged my knees to my chest in anticipation.

'There's a dress rehearsal soon,' said Mum. 'You'll enjoy that.'

'But won't it be really scary?' I wondered. I'd only stood in the wings of the stage with Jessie before – not actually *danced* on it.

'You'll love it,' Mum hugged me, then she tucked me up under the duvet and kissed me goodnight. 'Once you get a taste of dancing on stage, you and Rose won't want to stop. Night night, darling.'

'Night,' I yawned.

And in the dusk of my bedroom, as I listened to Myrtha's purry snores, I hoped that now she was safely home, all the unlucky thirteen stuff was right behind me.

Chapter Fifteen

The next Saturday before Extras, I raced into the ballet wardrobe to see Jessie.

'Just the person,' Jessie announced. 'Come and see these.'

Instead of being spread with fabrics and threads, Jessie's worktable was covered in pages from the newspaper. I looked at them.

'That's us!' I exclaimed.

They were the photos from the photocall.

'There's Karina and Veronica,' I pointed.

'And that's me and Rose!'

'I know,' Jessie said. 'I've cut them out so you can keep them.'

'Thanks!' I sighed. 'I'll take them to show the others . . .'

'You don't need to,' Jessie said. 'Miss Marion's already put up copies on the notice board.'

She helped me to carefully fold the newspaper pages and put them in my ballet bag.

'You can keep them in your special tin when you get home,' she said. 'But come on now – it's time for your class!'

'Ooops,' I said, heading for the door. 'See you after the rehearsal!'

'No, you won't,' Jessie said. 'You'll see me straight after class for your costume fitting – all of you will.'

Of course! How could I have forgotten?

101

Everyone was gathered around the notice board, looking at the pictures from the newspaper.

'Have you seen them?' Rose asked.

I nodded. 'Jessie's cut them out for me to keep – they're in here.' I pointed to my bag.

'Anyone can go and buy a newspaper,' Veronica sneered, glaring at me and then storming off to the studio for class.

'She thinks she should have been in a photo on her own,' Karina explained.

I smiled. If only Veronica could be more like Karina . . .

As soon as class was over, Jessie, Adam and Belinda arrived with Amber and Mary. Amber and Mary were dressers. They helped the dancers get into their costumes and put on headdresses and hairpieces. They'd come to the studio with a rack of costumes. *Our* costumes for the ballet!

'OK,' said Adam, looking at a piece of paper. 'When I call out your name could you go over to Belinda and Jessie, who'll give you your costume.'

Adam looked serious.

One by one, our names were called. Every costume was gorgeous. And Amber and Mary were so fast at helping us get changed. All around the room, everyone started to twirl and dance. We couldn't help it because the costumes felt so good. After all, they were made for dancing. And in less than two weeks we'd be wearing them on stage!

Miss Marion and Jessie soon got us to stand still though, so that tiny adjustments could be made to make sure the costumes were a perfect fit.

I didn't ever want to take mine off. But in the end, we all had to and the costumes were taken away, ready to be made exactly right for the dress rehearsal.

'Rehearsal in here in fifteen minutes, girls,' Miss Marion said.

'See you later, Jessie,' I waved as Rose and I headed off to the changing room.

We could hear music coming from one of the other studios.

'Come on,' said Rose. 'Let's see if we can peek through the door and see what's going on.'

There was a small window in the door and we stood on tiptoe to peer through. The dancers of the Grand Ballet were finishing their class. I saw my mum and dad, doing their centre work, exactly like we'd just done. But they were concentrating hard and didn't notice us. So, after a while, Rose and I headed off.

Back in the changing room, the corner where Rose and I had left our stuff was a mess. My clothes were everywhere. Worse, the newspaper pages that Jessie had saved for me were crumpled all over the floor.

'What's happened?' I said, picking up my things.

'Oh, Tilly!' Rose sighed.

'Come on,' said Karina. 'We'll help.'

She and Rose started scooping up my clothes as I concentrated on the cuttings.

'How did this happen?' I wondered.

'Huh,' said Veronica. 'It was probably that cat that hangs around here – it's always in the way.'

'Giselle doesn't do things like this!' I snapped. 'It couldn't have been her!'

'Suit yourself,' Veronica said. 'But you'd better hurry up or you'll miss the start of the rehearsal.' And she marched out of the room.

'Come on,' said Rose, hooking her arm in mine when we'd finished.

'But why was only my stuff messed up?' I sighed.

'And why,' pointed out Karina, 'was Veronica in the room on her own when I got here . . . ?'

I knew Veronica didn't like me much. But could she really be the one who'd trashed my stuff?

Chapter Sixteen

There was no time to worry about what had happened. With less than two weeks until the world premiere of *Promenade*, we were rehearsing nearly every day. Then, at last, it was the day of the dress rehearsal. All our hard work was going to be put to the test!

Rose and I had the day off school so we could spend it at the theatre. We arrived really early and did a warm-up class with the Grand Ballet. Then Miss Marion took the Extras backstage and led us to a big dressing room. There was another smaller one for the boys.

'This is where you'll be changing while the ballet is on,' she explained. 'And Amber and Mary will be helping you.'

We all looked around excitedly. It was like being a proper dancer!

'Your costumes are on the rail here,' Amber said. 'Come on – let's get you ready.'

We could hear the orchestra warming up as the costumes were handed out and everyone started changing.

'Where's mine?' I asked, looking at the empty rack.

'That's strange . . .' sighed Mary. 'Don't worry – I'll phone Jessie.'

But Jessie hadn't a clue where my costume was. All around me, the Extras were putting the finishing touches to their hair and make-up. And I still wasn't dressed.

'If I don't find my costume soon, I'll miss the rehearsal!' I exclaimed to Rose.

'You might have to dance in your leotard,' Miss Marion warned. 'But go and have your hair done while I get the others on the stage – I'll be back when I can!'

How was this possible? This was my first chance to dance on stage and it was all going wrong. I shivered in my leotard as my hair was plaited. Overhead, the orchestra was getting louder and louder. They were obviously nearly ready to start!

But just then Jessie arrived.

'Found it! It was in the wrong dressing room! Quick! Let's get you on that stage!'

We found Miss Marion in the wings.

'Thank heavens,' she said when we told her where my costume had been. 'Now get to your places.'

Rose and I joined Charlie and Cynthia and then the orchestra began. The music sounded amazing. I could feel myself swaying to the beat.

'Ready?' asked Charlie.

I gulped. What if I went wrong? Or if I fell over again? I could make the whole ballet a disaster!

Rose squeezed my hand as the first dancers entered the stage. I tried to see where Mum and Dad were. Dad was playing the part of a grumpy man who kept telling everyone off. He was really funny in it. And Mum was in the wings on the other side of the stage. She was playing the part of a glamorous lady and was wearing the most gorgeous dress.

'It's nearly our turn,' Rose whispered.

I gulped again. One, two, three . . . two, two, three . . . three, two, three . . . we were on stage at last. For the first time in our lives, Rose and I were dancing on a real stage!

I loved every minute of it – and you could tell the others felt the same. Everyone was grinning and their eyes sparkled with the excitement. Mitzi stopped the dancing a couple of times to ask people to move to different places on the stage. And the conductor asked questions about the speed of some of the music so that the orchestra wasn't playing too fast.

When the ballet was over, Miss Marion even rehearsed our curtain calls (that's the curtseys at the end). And Mitzi came over to tell us that we'd done a good job!

'That was totally amazing,' Veronica announced, leading the way back to the dressing room. 'I think Mitzi was very impressed with us older dancers.'

Rose rolled her eyes. 'She's so full of herself,' she whispered.

I giggled. 'I'm surprised anyone else is needed on stage. After all, she thinks she could do every part.'

Some of the others started to giggle too.

Veronica turned round and glared. 'What's so funny?' she barked. 'Huh! You're all so unprofessional!'

But that just made us all collapse into giggles. And Veronica stormed to the dressing room in a huff.

Veronica's behaviour was starting to really annoy me. I told Mum all about it later, over supper.

'Sounds like the poor girl's getting anxious about the performance,' she said.

'Perhaps,' I sighed and then I felt butterflies in my own tummy.

It was only two days until opening night!

Chapter Seventeen

The next day, Rose and I arrived early at the Grand Theatre.

'I can't believe it's the last rehearsal already,' Helen said

'And on Friday we'll do our first performance!' Rose exclaimed.

We said goodbye to Helen and then sped off to the changing room. Karina was already there.

Usually, I take my ballet bag with me to class each time but because there'd been so many rehearsals, I'd left it in the changing room. I grabbed it from the hook and started to fish out my stuff.

'Yuck!' I said.

My leotard was wet. And so were my tights. Even my just-in-case stuff was damp. But, weirdly, my shoes weren't.

'How did *that* happen?' Rose wondered.

'Who can have done this?' I gasped. 'And what can I wear for the rehearsal?'

'You can borrow these tights,' Rose offered.

'And I've got another leotard,' Karina said, pulling it from her own bag. 'It might be a bit big but it will do.'

'Thanks so much,' I sighed, quickly changing. 'What would I do without you?'

In the studio, Veronica was already warming up at the *barre*. She really did want to show Miss Marion how keen she was! As she pulled up from her *pliés*, she glanced round at us and glared. She stopped dancing and came over.

'That's not your leotard,' she hissed.

'It's Karina's,' I explained. 'Mine was all wet in my bag . . .'

'Huh!' she said. 'I bet the cat weed all over it. Serve you right for letting it come into the dressing room all the time.'

Why was she always blaming Giselle? I opened my mouth to say that she would never do something like that. But I didn't get the chance.

'Boys and girls,' Miss Marion said, 'let's all warm up and then we can begin the rehearsal.'

Afterwards, I told Jessie what had happened.

'She can't blame Giselle,' I sighed.

'Of course she can't,' Jessie said. 'Just try to ignore her. Maybe she doesn't like cats.'

I looked at Giselle, who was curled up asleep in her basket, and shrugged. How could anyone not like Giselle?

I sighed, putting the wet clothes on the worktable. 'But how did my leotard get wet? It was inside my bag! And it was only my clothes – nothing else.'

'It is a bit strange,' Jessie agreed. 'And a bit suspicious ...'

'You think someone did it *on purpose*?' I said.

Jessie shook her head. 'I don't know. Perhaps it was just an accident and someone spilled water on it by mistake. Sometimes people are too embarrassed to own up to things, aren't they?'

Hmmm, I thought. 'Actually, I think

I left my leotard and tights on the peg. Not in my bag.'

'There you are then,' Jessie said. 'Perhaps they fell on the floor and someone spilled water on them, then hid them in your bag to cover it up.'

'Perhaps,' I said. 'But I'm getting fed up with all these bad things that keep happening to me . . .'

Jessie gave me a hug. 'I know, so I thought you might like this' She handed me a small blue box. 'Go on – open it!'

It was like a small jewellery box and, when I flicked open the top, there was the most gorgeous silver ballerina charm sparkling inside.

'Wow, it's gorgeous!' I exclaimed.

'I thought you'd like it,' Jessie smiled. 'It's to wish you luck on opening night.'

I jumped up and gave her a hug.

'Oh, thank you! I wish I could wear it on stage . . .' But no one was allowed to wear jewellery on stage.

'I've thought of that,' Jessie said, tapping her nose. 'I'm going to sew it into your costume − so you *can* take it on stage with you.'

I grinned and stroked the ballerina. 'This is the best bit of luck I could have!'

Chapter Eighteen

Rose and I went to school on Friday morning but it was hard to concentrate, knowing what was going to happen later on. At last Mum and Dad came to fetch us. We were off to the theatre to the world premiere of Mitzi's ballet.

'Good luck, you two!' said Bob, as we arrived at the Stage Door.

'See you in the wings!' said Mum and Dad.

We nodded and headed off down the

corridor. People were everywhere. Dancers, musicians, stage hands – everyone was getting ready for the performance.

Miss Marion was going to give the Extras a short class, so we could warm up before the performance. Veronica arrived as we were getting changed.

'Do you think she's been crying?' Rose whispered to me. 'Her eyes are all red!'

I sneaked a peek at her as I put on my shoes.

'I don't think so . . .' I started to say. But before I could finish, Veronica let out a huge sneeze.

'Bless you!' Karina said. 'Hey – are you OK?'

Veronica blew her nose. 'I've got a cold . . .'

'Poor you,' Rose said.

'That's not fair,' I agreed.

Veronica looked rotten. And I think we all felt sorry for her.

'I just hope I don't sneeze on stage,' Veronica said.

'You'll be fine,' said Karina.

'Well, I'll have to be,' Veronica sniffed. 'Like they say, the show must go on!'

Class was really short – just *barre* work. And afterwards, Miss Marion took us to our dressing rooms back stage. I searched through the rail with the costumes on it.

'Mine's there,' I said with a sigh of relief.

Inside the costume, where it couldn't be seen once it was on, Jessie had sewn a label that said GRAND BALLET COMPANY. Ballet: *Promenade*. Dancer: Tilly Tippington. Just like in the costumes of the dancers in the Grand Ballet!

'Is the charm there?' Rose asked. She'd wanted to see it ever since I'd told her about the lucky silver ballerina that Jessie had given to me.

We peeked inside – and there it was. The little silver charm, sewn in carefully with tiny stitches.

'It's gorgeous,' Rose sighed.

I stroked the ballerina with my finger. It felt cool and smooth. And lucky!

Suddenly there was an announcement over the speaker in the dressing room. It was the stage manager.

'Good evening, ladies and gentlemen. One hour to curtain up, please. One hour to curtain up!'

I gripped Rose's hand and felt the butterflies begin to flutter around my tummy again.

'Right,' said Amber. 'Time to get

everyone's hair ready and then you can get dressed.'

In sixty minutes, we were going to be on stage . . .

Jessie popped into the dressing room just before we were ready to go.

'Don't you look fantastic,' she said, admiring us. 'Look at your hair!'

We were standing there in our bright costumes with our wild, wired plaits tied in neon coloured ribbons. It felt amazing.

'Thanks again for my good luck charm,' I said with a smile.

'Ten minutes, ladies and gentlemen,' announced the stage manager. We could hear the musicians in the orchestra pit warming up. 'Overture and beginners on stage, please.'

'That's you!' Jessie grinned.

We held hands in pairs as we walked towards the stage.

'Hey, Veronica,' I called. 'Your hair!'

Veronica spun round, panic across her face.

'What is it?'

'Your ribbon's come loose,' Rose pointed out.

'Oh no!' Veronica looked like she might cry.

'Don't worry,' Amber said. 'I'll sort it.'

'Phew,' Karina said. 'Good job you spotted that before she got on stage!'

Chapter Nineteen

'Good luck,' said Mum, as soon as we were back stage. She looked beautiful in her red and pink costume.

'Enjoy yourselves!' said Dad, popping a kiss on my cheek. 'See you at the end!'

Mum and Dad went off to their opening positions.

'Ready, you two?' Charlie asked us.

We nodded. 'We can't wait!' said Rose.

From the wings, we could see the stage but the audience was still hidden behind the curtain. You could hear the buzz of everyone chatting and the musicians trilling through their notes. Suddenly, it all went quiet.

'That must be the lights going down,' I whispered to Rose, squeezing her hand.

There was total hush. All around us, dancers stood in position. Then we heard the opening bars of music . . . slowly, the curtain went up.

The first dancers entered the stage. It was really strange to see them from the wings and not from the front of the studio. I'd seen the steps so many times, I could almost dance them all myself. La, de, da da the music went − it was our cue.

Gallop and point, gallop and hop. Rose and I were actually on stage! It felt magical with my costume swishing around me and everyone dancing their hearts out.

The scenery was so life-like I felt as if I was actually in a park. We greeted all the other people as we danced past and took in the stories they were telling.

Miss Marion had told us we needed to make sure the people in the seats at the back could see what we were doing so any facial expressions had to be vivid – almost exaggerated – to tell our stories. I tried to remember everything we had been taught. I pointed my toes hard and bent my knees low. I raised my head high and smiled. But with the bright lights you almost couldn't see the people in the audience – they were just a blur.

Then came the moment when the adult dancers did their solos. Mum was amazing as she always is in her graceful, flowing dress. She looked like she was floating across the stage. Dad made everyone laugh as his grumpy old man getting irritated with the children in the park. He kept pulling silly faces and tottering around as if he was going to fall over. Then, like a gymnast, he managed to bounce off in the opposite direction, spinning like a top. He was incredible.

But then, suddenly, I heard from the music that we were almost at the end. How could it have gone so quickly? In rehearsals, we'd gone through everything in such detail, I hadn't realised how fast the ballet would seem in a performance.

One by one, just as the stage had filled at the beginning, each group of dancers left the park and went home. The lights on stage dimmed, as the sky would get darker at dusk. The park keeper looked at his watch and closed the gates across the stage and that was it – the ballet had ended.

'That was brilliant!' whispered Rose as we hugged each other in the wings.

The curtain was falling but the applause from the audience had already begun.

'Listen!' I said.

All around us, dancers were grinning, pleased that the ballet had gone without a mistake. We hurried to the back of the stage. The curtain was coming back up again and the lights were flooding the rest of the theatre. It was time for our curtain call!

One by one, the lines of dancers took their bows and curtseys. Then the soloists took their turns. The applause was loud and enthusiastic. Finally, just as we'd been taught in rehearsal, we skipped onto the stage and did our *reverence*. The applause carried on and on. I didn't want it to stop. But, as we'd rehearsed, we came up from our curtseys and bows, smiled and returned to our positions at the back of the stage.

Still the applause came. I tried to see Helen and Miss Marion in the audience but couldn't make them out amongst the sea of people. Mitzi came on stage and then we clapped her as well as the audience.

And then she turned round and clapped us!

We were all about to step forward and take another bow with Mitzi when some men appeared on stage. They were giving flowers to some of the soloists. I'd seen this so many times from the audience but, when you're on stage, it's even more special. Then the men came back on stage with more flowers. Only this time, they walked passed the soloists and came through to the back line where the Extras were. Karina was given flowers. So was Veronica. And then Rose and I were given some little posies of the prettiest flowers ever.

'Thank you!' I gasped.

We all took one more *reverence* and then the curtain fell. Our first performance was finally over.

I looked at the flowers. There was a note on them:

With love from Jessie and everyone in the ballet wardrobe xxx

'That was the best night of my life!' I said to Rose.

'Me too,' grinned Rose.

'Well done, you two.' We got a hug from behind. It was Mum.

'I am so proud of you both,' said Jessie, rushing on stage. 'I watched it all from the audience and you were wonderful. Perfect!'

Dad lifted us both up, Rose and me, one in each arm and twirled us around.

'Was I OK?' I asked when he finally put us down.

'OK?' Dad exclaimed. 'You were brilliant, both of you!'

Chapter Twenty

Helen took me and Rose to the ballet wardrobe the next day.

'I can't tell you how amazing it was to see them on stage,' Helen told Jessie.

'I know!' Jessie agreed. 'They were like real dancers, weren't they?'

Rose and I grinned as we played with Giselle, who was chasing a cotton reel.

'I was really worried I might make a mistake,' I said. 'But we'd rehearsed so much it didn't happen.'

'And looking out from the wings is even better than watching from the audience,' Rose said.

I knew exactly what she meant.

'Miss Marion said she was really pleased with us,' I said.

'She said we were good,' added Rose.

'You were! I can't imagine being able to jump as high as you two,' sighed Adam.

Just then, the door opened. It was Belinda, carrying the newspaper.

'Exactly the people I wanted to see,' she announced, placing the opened paper on the worktable in front of us. 'Look!'

It was a photograph of Mum in the paper. 'Premiere of ballet makes the Grand grander!' it said.

'It's the review of last night,' said Helen.

'Let's see,' I gasped.

The room fell silent as we crowded round.

'*Promenade* is an exciting ballet from the world-famous choreographer Mitzi Morgan ... outstanding performances were given by all the dancers ...' Jessie read aloud. 'A particular treat was to see the young pupils who train with the Grand Ballet. Their excellence showed that today's students are sure to be tomorrow's stars!'

'Wow!' we exclaimed, jumping up and down with excitement.

'You'd better take that with you down to the dressing room,' Jessie suggested. 'I'm sure the others will want to see it.'

So we did. In fact, we stuck it on the mirror to make sure nobody could miss it.

'Isn't that fantastic?' Karina said when she saw it.

'You should all be proud of yourselves,' said Mary as she wheeled in the costumes.

Phew, I thought, checking mine was

there. I stroked the charm hidden inside. That ballerina had brought me good luck. I would never worry about unlucky thirteen again.

'Achooo!' Veronica arrived, still looking red-nosed from her cold.

'Hey, Veronica,' I said, thinking how funny it was that all the bad things stopped happening to me just when Veronica had got this cold. 'Are you feeling any better?'

'You did really well last night,' Rose said. 'Especially as you were ill.'

'Er, thanks,' Veronica said, blowing her nose. 'I'm a bit better today.'

'It's such bad luck that you've got a cold now,' Karina said. 'But have you seen the review in the paper?'

Veronica peered at the mirror. A smile slowly spread across her face. I looked at

Rose. It must have been one of the first times any of us had seen Veronica smile.

'How cool is that?' Veronica said. 'Actually . . .' She put her coat on the hook and sat down. 'Actually, I thought you were all really good. Er . . . thanks for telling me about my ribbon. If I'd gone on stage with it loose, I'd have let the Extras down.'

I could hardly believe it. None of us could. Veronica was being nice! *What had happened to her?*

'Come on, ladies,' said Mary. 'It's time to start getting ready for the matinee.'

'It's just like being real dancers, isn't it?' I said, joining the queue to get my hair plaited and wired up.

Rose nodded.

'But we *are* real dancers,' Karina said. 'After all, we're performing on stage at the Grand Theatre!'

We all giggled.

'Karina's right,' said Veronica. 'We're dancers with the Grand Ballet!'

Rose and I jumped up and down. Our dream was coming true.

'Then we'd better get ready for our next performance!' I announced.

And I knew right then that I would become a dancer whatever it took!

Look out for more adventures starring
Tilly Tiptoes and all her friends
at the Grand Ballet . . .

Tilly Tiptoes
and the
Grand Surprise

The dancers of the Grand Ballet are
practising for the opening night of *Giselle*.
But objects are going missing from the
theatre, from bits of costume to leotards
and legwarmers. Is there a naughty fairy
up to no good, or maybe even a ghost?
Tilly tries to find out . . .

Tilly Tiptoes and the Gala Show

The Grand Ballet are getting ready
for a Gala performance of *Cinderella*, but
Tilly has other things on her mind. She has
a ballet exam next week, and though she's
tried everything, she just can't remember
the steps. Does this mean the end
of her dancing dreams?

To find out more about *Tilly Tiptoes*,

as well as discover other exciting books, visit:

www.catnippublishing.co.uk